Poison Pages

by Michael Dahl

Illustrated by Martín Blanco

STONE ARCH BOOKS
a capstone imprint

Library of Doom is published by Stone Arch Books,
A Capstone imprint
1710 Roe Crest Drive
North Mankato, Minnesota 56003
www.mycapstone.com

Library of Congress Cataloging-in-Publication
Data is available on the Library of
Congress website.

ISBN: 978-1-4965-5527-4 (library binding)
ISBN: 978-1-4965-5533-5 (paperback)
ISBN: 978-1-4965-5539-7 (eBook PDF)

Summary: The Librarian works to save people
trapped between the pages of a deadly book.

Designer: Brent Slingsby

Photo credits
Design Element: Shutterstock: Shebeko.

Printed and bound in the USA.
010369F17

Table of Contents

The girl looks into
the distance.

She can see a faraway
shape. It looks like a
giant wave.

"The page is turning,"
says the Librarian.

THE LIBRARIAN

Real name: unknown
Parents: unknown
Birthplace/birthdate: unknown
Weaknesses: water, crumbs, dirty fingers
Strengths: speed reading, ability to fly, martial arts

THE LIBRARY

The Library of Doom is the world's largest collection of strange and dangerous books. Each generation, a new Librarian is chosen to serve as guardian. The Librarian's duty is to keep the books from falling into the hands of those who would use them for evil.

The location of the Library of Doom is unknown. Its shelves sit partially hidden underground. Some sections form a maze. It is full of black holes. This means someone might walk down a hallway in the Library and not realize they are traveling thousands of miles. One hallway could start somewhere under the Atlantic Ocean and end inside the caves of the Himalayas.

There are entries to the Library scattered all over the earth. But there are few exits. Sometimes villains find their way into the vast collection, but the Librarian always finds them out!

— From *The Atlas Cryptical*, compiled by Orson Drood, 5th official Librarian

CHAPTER ONE

THE EMPTY SEAT

The city is gray and cold. Rain falls from an angry sky.

A young girl holds an umbrella and waits for the bus to take her home.

The bus arrives full of sad, sleepy passangers.

The girl finds a place to sit, but there is a small, square shadow on the seat.

"Someone forgot their book," the girl says to herself.

She picks up the shadowy book and looks at the cover. Weird letters spell out **The Lost Readers**.

When she turns a page, the girl sees a **picture** of a gray girl waiting for a bus. The gray girl climbs onto a gray bus and finds a seat.

On the next page is another picture.
It shows the gray girl's seat, but this
time the girl is gone.

Suddenly, on the real bus, the real
girl is gone too.

Only the **shadowy** book is
left behind.

CHAPTER TWO

THE ENDLESS FLOOR

The girl is no longer on the bus. She is outside. She is standing on a wide, flat floor. The floor is `endless`.

The endless floor is covered with black shapes.

She bends down and sees that the shapes are painted on the floor.

"Letters," says the girl.

"I am inside the book," she says to herself.

In the distance, the girl sees another shape. It is a man walking toward her.

The girl is frightened. She turns to walk away.

"Stop!" shouts the man. "Take one more step, and it will be your last!"

CHAPTER THREE

THE LOST READERS

"Who are you?" asks the girl.

"I am the Librarian," says the man.
"You have been taken by the book.
Along with the others."

"Others?" says the girl.

The girl looks and now she can see other shapes.

Men, women, and children crowd around the **edges** of the endless floor.

"Who are they?" asks the girl.

"The lost readers," says the Librarian. "We are all inside the pages of the book."

The girl takes a step forward.

"I told you not to move," said the Librarian. "Do you want to end up like that?"

He points to a **figure** lying near them.

CHAPTER FOUR

THE POISON PATH

The girl looks down. She was about to step on one of the <u>letters</u>.

"The letters are made of poison ink," says the Librarian.

"If you touch the poison, you will become part of the book forever."

"I've never heard of a poison book," says the girl.

"It is not an ordinary book," he says. "It comes from the Library of Doom."

"Follow me," he says. "Put your feet where I put mine."

Carefully, they walk across the **endless** floor.

"Let go!" the girl shouts.

One of the figures has grabbed
her foot.

CHAPTER FIVE

TRAPPED ON THE PAGE

"Why?" gasps the figure. "Why?"

The Librarian bends down and frees the girl's foot from the figure's **grasp**.

"He was poisoned by a question mark and cannot stop asking questions," says the Librarian.

The girl looks into the distance. She can see a faraway shape. It looks like a giant wave.

"The page is turning," says the Librarian.

The girl and the man race across the **vast floor**.

"Who are they?" asks the girl.

She sees some people tightly wrapped
with strips of paper.

They cannot move their arms or legs.
She hears them **moan**.

"Those are the library bound," says the Librarian. "We cannot stop to help them."

The girl looks behind her. The giant wave is **growing** closer.

CHAPTER SIX

OVER THE EDGE

The Librarian suddenly stops. They are standing at the edge of the page.

Below them is a great **darkness**.

"You must jump," says the Librarian.

"But there's nothing there," the girl says.

"Trust me," says the Librarian.

The **giant** paper is getting closer and closer.

"All right," says the girl.

She closes her eyes. She takes a deep
breath and jumps.

The **wind** rushes past her body.

Bump!

The girl opens her eyes. She is back
on the bus.

She looks down at the book and sees
a picture of the Librarian.

Why didn't he jump? the girl wonders.

At the bottom of the page she sees
the words: There are more lost readers
who **need my help**.

THE END

Notes from the Librarian

There are books in the Library of Doom. Some get power by sucking victims into them. The more victims, the stronger the books grow.

I know how deadly these books are. I was once their victim. Before I became the Librarian, I worked as a page. One of my duties was to check on the Venomous Volume each morning.

One day, I was careless handling the book. A long, poisonous tongue lashed out from its pages. It stung my hand. I was in the Library's sickroom for three months. I still carry the scar. The experience taught me to never underestimate the power of evil words.

The poison books, like the one from this adventure, are the worst of them. After I rescued the girl, I put the books in a Kaku time bubble. The bubble changes its location every day.

A Page from the Library of Doom

Letters

- Cambodia has the world's longest alphabet with seventy-four letters.

- The world's shortest alphabet is used in the Solomon Islands of the South Pacific. It has only eleven letters.

- The Hawaiian alphabet is the next shortest with only twelve letters.

- The most common letter in English is E.

- W is the only letter in English that has more than one syllable.

- In almost every language on Earth, the word for "mother" begins with the letter M.

The Hawaiian Alphabet

A E I O U H

K L M N P W

About the Author

Michael Dahl is the prolific author of the bestselling *Goodnight Baseball* picture book and more than two hundred other books for children and young adults. He has won the AEP Distinguished Achievement Award three times for his nonfiction, a Teachers' Choice Award from *Learning* magazine, and a Seal of Excellence from the Creative Child Awards. Dahl currently lives in Minneapolis, Minnesota.

About the Illustrator

Martín Blanco was born in Argentina and studied drawing and painting at the Fine Arts University of Buenos Aires. He is currently a freelance illustrator and lives in Barcelona, Spain, where he is working on films and comic books. Blanco loves to read, especially thrillers and horror. He also enjoys soccer, the Barcelona football team, and playing the drums with his friends.

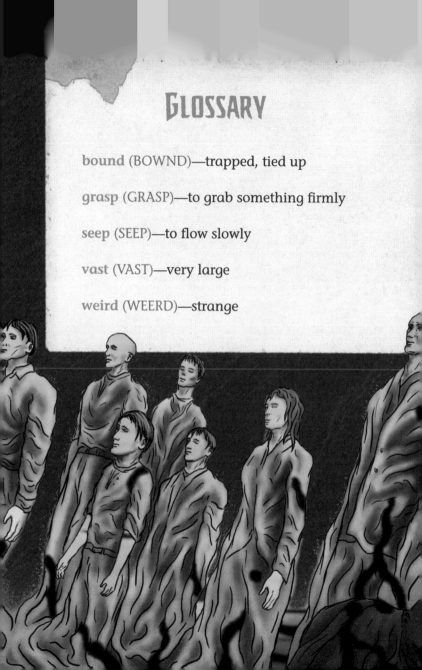

GLOSSARY

bound (BOWND)—trapped, tied up

grasp (GRASP)—to grab something firmly

seep (SEEP)—to flow slowly

vast (VAST)—very large

weird (WEERD)—strange

DISCUSSION QUESTIONS

1. If you could go inside a book and enter its story, which book would you choose? Why?

2. When the giant page is turning, the Librarian tells the girl to trust him and jump. What do you think would've happened if she had not trusted him?

3. The Librarian enters *The Lost Readers* to rescue the girl. Have you ever had a friend help you out during a hard time? Were you ever a good friend to someone who needed your help?

WRITING PROMPTS

1. What would happen if you found a mysterious book on your way to school? What would it look like? Would it be magical? Write down your adventure.

2. At the end of the story, the Librarian stayed behind to help other lost readers. Write a paragraph telling us how he helped another person escape from the book.

3. Pretend you are the person that grabbed the girl's leg on page 27. What's going through your mind in that situation? Rewrite the scene from your point of view.

Building the Library

Some words from author Michael Dahl

I've always fantasized about shrinking down and living inside a book. Like *The Hobbit* or one of *The Chronicles of Narnia*. But what if my new adventures did not have a happy ending? What if I got eaten by orcs or stung by giant spiders? What if I was trapped inside forever? That's what gave me the idea for this story.

The idea about adding poison to the story came from an alarming experience I had. Many years ago I visited friends down in Texas. We were walking through their neighborhood, and I was goofing off. I plucked a purple flower from a nearby bush and popped it in my mouth. Luckily I spit it out.

Later, I learned the bush was an oleander. If I had chewed or swallowed that flower, I would have been poisoned — or worse! Ever since, I've always had a healthy respect, and a curiosity, about poisons.

EXPLORE THE ENTIRE LIBRARY OF DOOM

THE DIGITAL ARCHIVES

DISCOVER MORE AT:

capstonekids.com

Authors and Illustrators
Videos and Contests
Games and Puzzles
Heroes and Villains